The Farmer's Boy

Barbara Willard

The Farmer's Boy

WITH ILLUSTRATIONS BY
ROBIN BELL CORFIELD

Julia MacRae Books
LONDON SYDNEY AUCKLAND JOHANNESBURG

Text copyright © 1991 Barbara Willard
Illustrations © 1991 Robin Bell Corfield
All rights reserved
First published in Great Britain 1991
by Julia MacRae
an imprint of the Random Century Group Ltd
20 Vauxhall Bridge Road London, SW1V 2SA

Random Century Australia (Pty) Ltd
20 Alfred Street Milsons Point Sydney, NSW 2061

Random Century New Zealand Ltd
PO Box 40-086 Glenfield Auckland 10 New Zealand

Random Century South Africa (Pty) Ltd
PO Box 337 Bergvlei 2012 South Africa

Typeset by BookEns Limited Baldock Herts
Printed and bound in Great Britain by
Butler & Tanner Ltd Frome and London

British Library Cataloguing in Publication Data
Willard, Barbara
The farmer's boy
I. Title
823.914 [J]
ISBN 1-85681-150-6

Contents

Chapter One

Because it was raining hard, Harry was on his way to school. With his hands deep in his jacket pockets and two sacks over his shoulders to keep some part of him dry, he went whistling across the forest. Every tree shone with wet; every leaf dripped; every yard of muddy track was a puddle. It was March, so the rain was not even a warm rain. Yet still Harry whistled as he trudged the five miles or so from his grandfather's farm to the Poor School near the church in the market town. Only when the weather made outdoor work impossible was Harry able to go to school as he longed to. He had worked for his grandfather since a little before his eighth birthday and now he was twelve. Farmer Hoad was certainly not a cruel master, but he could not understand why Harry, the farmer's boy, had determined to be a farmer's boy who could read and write and count his money.

"How'll I know how much I got, else?" demanded Harry of his grandfather, time and time again.

"It never come hard to me," the old man replied, winking. "Not that I had much, ever."

But Harry would not laugh.

Harry's sister Sarah, the oldest of the family and the only one besides him left at home, also disapproved, though she had learnt from her grandmother how to read and write at least a little.

"Better watch out," she said in a voice of solemn warning, one day when Harry had been talking and talking about school. "Anytime, if you don't watch out, you c'd find yourself halfway to a scholar."

"Any'un's the better for a bit o' knowing," said Harry.

"Whoever went and give you such ideas?"

"Mr Kingham - who else?"

"And why wouldn't he? He's a teacher, en't he? You're naun but a farmer's boy and so you'll stay till you grow to be a farmer. You're too old now for schooling. See you do your learning about home, for Grandda' can't live for ever."

That was not the first or the only time Sarah had spoken so. But their grandfather must live much longer or the farm might never be Harry's.

There was one place on the way to school where, if the light was right, it was possible for the merest tick in time to see the sea. It hung between two sloping lines of the downs, no bigger than a raindrop might appear close at hand. He saw it most often on his way home, when the rain had almost always stopped and the sky cleared. But he always looked back, rain or no, when he reached that point, just to make sure that the long swooping line of the downs still stood as they had stood for thousands of years, holding back the sea that might otherwise have rushed in from the channel and swamped the country-side. It was at this point, too, that the forest seemed to stretch for ever into every point of the compass, hill and valley, woodland and heathland, trickling water and still pond . . .

Now Harry began to hurry through the rain. Far off on a different track he saw a boy on a fat pony. That was Harry's neighbour and enemy, Sam Blagden, the son of Ranger Blagden - and he was Grandda's enemy. Sam was able to go to school any day of the week and the worst of that was that he hated it. He was much farther on his way than Harry, so from a fast walk Harry changed to a jog-trot and later to a run. He came up the hill to the school in the last nick of time. Mrs Kingham, the master's wife, was standing in the porch, vigorously ringing the bell. Two very small girls dashed towards her from the far side of the cobbled street, and she held out her hand to them, smiling as they paused to bob to her before running into the school.

Mrs Kingham saw Harry panting up the last few yards, and she held the door for him.

"A splendid wet day, Harry! I'm glad to see you. The weather has been too fine for learning, hasn't it?"

"Yes, ma'am," said Harry, breathless and grinning. If Mr Kingham was the wisest man on earth, Mrs Kingham was the kindest woman. She taught the girls while her husband was dealing with the boys.

"Wait now, Harry!" She pulled the soaking wet sacks from his shoulders. A rack of odd clothes that could be handed out to any pupil arriving drenched was one of the Kinghams' good ideas. "Take off that jacket - here's one that may fit you well enough. I'll hang yours to dry. And take off your boots when you get into the schoolroom - you know where to find dry slippers."

He did know. A line of slippers of various sizes always stood by the schoolroom hearth, to be borrowed as needed. Harry had never known his mother, and his sister Sarah certainly did not pamper him. Mrs Kingham, therefore, appeared to him as some kind of dream lady who could do no wrong. When he came to school he missed his dinner, and somehow Sarah had never felt a need to supply him with a packet of bread and cold bacon, or cheese and onion - it was Mrs Kingham who did that as soon as she discovered that he was going hungry. Sometimes Harry allowed himself a dream of snowy weather which would catch him when he was already at school and become so severe so fast that he would be allowed to stay with Mr and Mrs Kingham until a thaw set in. I'd learn a whole bookful of things, he told himself, when he contemplated this enchanting vision.

As Harry went into the boys' schoolroom that wet March morning, he saw Sam Blagden and Sam saw him. Harry made for the hearth, where there were as many as four or five pairs of slippers left over from the borrowing of earlier arrivals.

As Harry reached for what looked like a proper sized pair, Sam's foot shot out and sent all the slippers flying in every direction across the floor. There was a bellow of laughter and instantly a dozen or so boys were chasing the slippers, kicking them as if towards a goal, jostling and shouting, the younger ones falling down as the bigger sort pushed them aside. Desks and benches were banged and shoved, scraping along the bare boards and crashing into one another with a booming and cracking that suggested there would soon be no two parts of anything left together. In no time, from knocking one another about with wild laughter, one or two started fighting, and then others joined in. They were far too occupied to see Mr Kingham enter and, without pausing, walk towards his desk and mount the small platform on which it stood. There was a ruler lying on the desk. He picked it up and brought it down with so sharp a report that there was instant silence.

"Put the room to rights," he ordered in a voice that did not need to be at all loud.

They fell to, quick and nervous, glancing at one another with silly grins, trying to sort out which desk went where, which stool with which desk. When it was done they stood, stifling giggles that were sheer fright. Nothing quite the same had happened to these pupils before and they were unsure how their master would deal with them. Mr Kingham was not a tall man, not broad shouldered or even stern in expression. His power lay in the fact that he seemed able always to see into their wicked young minds and to deal with them in ways of his own that left them helpless.

When the silence was complete, Mr Kingham looked at Harry.

"Sit down, Hoad. Blagden - pick up a pair of slippers and put them on for him. Kneel down and do it properly."

There was a swift titter as Sam, scowling and shaking with temper, did as he was told. The one way in which he was able to get a bit of his own back was to choose odd shoes - the left too big, the right too small and he managed to hurt quite a lot as he did what he had been instructed to do.

If Mr Kingham was aware of what was going on, he gave no sign of it, waiting without word or movement until he was ready.

"Stand by your desks," he said then, in his firm voice. "Complete silence, if you please."

He waited until he got it, until the last painful giggle had died. Then, without further delay, he folded his hands, bowed his head and proceeded with morning prayers.

Along with all the rest, Harry bowed his head, put his hands together and closed his eyes. But he could not resist a quick look at Mr Kingham, letting up one lid cunningly to do so. Mr Kingham's voice might not be loud, yet it had the power of some mysterious drum, solemn, dedicated, utterly sincere. Like his wife, he offered Harry an ideal. He was a good man ready always to work for others, as Harry already knew. Perhaps this meant that he found too little time for laughter, but that was a price that had to be paid.

"Amen," said Mr Kingham.

"Amen," they all replied, though in a subdued and rather careful fashion.

"Be seated," the master said.

And seated they were.

Chapter Two

. . . AND BACK AGAIN

By mid-afternoon the rain had stopped; by the time Harry set out for home the sun had recovered about half the sky. Westward, a bright gold edging to the galloping line of the downs was kept in its place by boulders of storm cloud the colour of slate. At that magical point where earlier in the day the wink of sea had been barely visible, there shone now a stab of blue that vanished almost as soon as Harry smiled to see it. The entire forest was shaking off the day's drenching. Catkins on hazel and birch, well past their best, hung out what remained and took new life from the rapidly descending sun. Snippets of green on the willows showed the speedy advance of the year; within a week they would be green all over. As Harry bounded downhill towards the crossing of the smallest river, now carrying his boots wrapped up in the sacks that had been dried by Mrs Kingham, he knew he might very well see the first daffodil of the year, which grew in a spot so sheltered it was always ahead of its fellows.

His brother Luke had first shown Harry that daffodil, in the very same year that disaster had caught him. That was already getting on for three years ago, but Harry had never got used to the certainty that he need not hope to see Luke ever again.

It was because of Luke, as well as because of school itself, that Harry was able to think of Mr and Mrs Kingham as his friends, however far above him. Their dedication to the care and causes of the forest dwellers had meant that they tried hard to save Luke as he stood accused. They had not given up till the very last, so that they had seemed almost like special parents. But they were not parents at all.

"It is God's will that we have no children of our own," Mrs Kingham had once said, with her warm smile. "He leaves us free to care for any that may need us. By the time we die we shall have had more children than may be counted!"

Now the daffodil was left behind and Harry had reached that place just short of home which was always a trouble to him. This was the moment when he could see the cottage looming where Sam Blagden lived with his father, the Ranger, and his half-sister, May, who kept house for them. Harry knew in his heart that May would one day have married Luke – he was sure she had looked at no one since he went. What it could have been like to have Sam for a relation by marriage, Harry had not let himself consider. For May was so different from Sam that it was hard to believe they came from the same father. If May had married Luke, and Luke had taken on Hoads Farm when his grandfather died, then that might well have satisfied Ranger Blagden. As it was, he was known to have different ideas.

"It's Hoads he want," Sarah had told Harry. "See if he don't try for it one day. That place o' his'n's just not good enough for the way he see himself."

All round the forest fringes there were small farms and holdings, but not all belonged to those who worked them. Years ago, all land had belonged to the king. As kings grew less powerful, the land became divided into manors under wealthy lords. All the forest was owned by a Lord of the Manor and those farmers who did not possess their lands for themselves and their heirs were the Lord's tenants. Grandda' was a tenant and when he died, if he had no heir to offer as the new tenant, the farm would go back to the Lord, who could give it where he chose – and why not to Ranger Blagden, already an employee? This was clearly a great worry to Sarah and she had passed on the worry to young Harry.

Harry hesitated now, as Rangers Cottage came into view. It was an ancient stone building, just as Hoads was, with a small-holding that grew vegetables and provided for several goats as well as hens. But Harry was looking towards the paddock, seeing Sam's fat pony and knowing, therefore, that Sam was home. There was a longer and more winding track he might have taken and avoided Rangers altogether. But he was already a little behind time, the cows would be waiting and fussing; and if the milking and feeding had to be done by Sarah, he would never hear the last of it. She had already told him more than once that he should set out for home at least an hour earlier, since farm duties could not wait. It would be easier later in the season, for then they would be out to grass instead of banging about in the yard. It had been a mild spring so far, good grass-growing weather. Harry could not bear to think of the cows kept waiting, but he also found it all too difficult to leave the school before the day's work ended – though he had Mr Kingham's assurance that this would be excused. There were five cows, which made them all the more difficult to manage, what with calving and finding enough winter milk. Because of the cows, Harry stuck to the shorter route past Rangers.

He skirted the ground where the hens were strutting and scratching. A robin was singing furiously from some unseen perch – then it ended with a screech and flew past Harry's left ear with such a beating of wings, he expected to feel it brush against his cheek. At the same moment, a handful of small stones scattered from above his head, striking like pins.

He heard Sam's high, almost evil laugh that was halfway to a bad-tempered donkey's bray. He must be somewhere over to the left, Harry decided, slightly above him, shouting and chanting one of the home-made verses he was always so proud of.

"Hoad, Hoad, son of a toad . . . More'f a ninny than any man know'd . . . Pick up what's sent 'un and get on thee road!"

At this Harry thought best to run. He was too slow to miss a great shower of clods hurled down from the bank where Sam was perched, his lurcher bitch, Dolly, barking furiously beside him. One clod hit Harry on the back of his neck, another struck him behind the knee. Then Sam must have changed direction and Harry was hit twice in the face. The more he dodged the more Sam found his target – and through it all Harry heard his enemy's braying laughter. Then the sound was much nearer. There was Sam, hopping about just ahead of Harry, jeering and yelling and making enough noise for three. The very thought of three Sam Blagdens made the hair prickle on Harry's scalp. He shivered – and then was instantly filled with hatred enough to make him strong.

He hurled himself at Sam and they went down together among the wildly cackling and scattering hens. They rolled over the rain-soaked ground, the dog leaping and barking around and over them. As they fell, a terrible stench rose up, for the clods Sam had hurled so successfully were balls of goat dung. The filth broke down and spread over their clothes before either boy was able to beat off the other. Rage and misery bolstered Harry's young muscles. He struck out wildly and viciously and caught Sam on the right ear – then grabbed the ear and hung on until Sam began to shriek and lash out without proper direction. Then, somehow managing a cruel twist of the ear, Harry chucked Sam away from him. His enemy flailed about for a second, yelling with pain, then lost his voice altogether as he smacked down, spread-eagled, his face in a filthy puddle.

For a moment Harry was very ready to forget about respecting a fallen enemy. He longed to kick Sam as he lay on the ground, to shove him back each time he struggled to find his feet on the slimy ground . . .

14

Someone called their names. Harry knew who it must be and he turned away, trying to run.

"Harry! Wait – do wait!"

Sam's sister, May, was coming across the yard as fast as she dared without slipping and falling in her turn.

"Get indoors, you!" she cried to Sam. "I'll have you under the pump, see if I don't – and let you choke for all I'd care! You're not fit for this world and that's the truth! Get in, wun't you? Do's I bid and smart about it!"

Harry had not stopped when May called, but thrust on his way, dreading what awaited him when he reached home – late for milking and covered head to foot in awful reeking muck. He could not hold back a stupid, blubbering cry. Tears at least cleared his face a bit. In the flurry he had lost his boots in their sacking parcel – another thing that was going to please Sarah.

May was now running after Harry.

"Wait, you great ninny, you!"

But she did not catch up with him till he was at the farm. He stopped dead, then. Sarah was coming from the milking shed, carrying two full pails on a yoke. Somewhere in the background, happy cows frisked and clattered round the yard.

There was nothing frisky about Sarah's attitude.

"Where've you bin, you lazy mawkin! Late again! Late for milking! When'll you learn cows can't be kep' waiting? So I can do your work, can I, whiles you get off learning to be smart!"

Between his angry sister and Sam's, Harry did not know where to turn. He stood with hunched shoulders, waiting for some final blow.

"All right, all right now!" May called to Sarah. "Leave him be and hear the tale. None o' his fault, I'd say."

"Oh, indeed! Whose, then, I'd like to ask."

"Who'd you think? Young Sam, who else? He's naun but a demon. Any knows that save his father."

Sarah had suddenly realised the state Harry was in.

"Look at'm! Will you just look? There's no place else for that jacket but the bonfire!"

May shrugged and turned her back on Sarah. "Come on now, Harry. Cheer up a bit. Your sister's busy. I'll see you fetched clean again. Come on, now – come on. There's no dirt can't be washed away. Come on wi' me, dear."

Now her voice was soft, warm, as it mostly was to Luke's youngest brother. Why couldn't she have been his sister instead of Sam's? Why wasn't Sarah more like her?

Now she had taken his filthy hand and was pulling him towards the house. The pump was by the kitchen door. Harry saw that his grandfather was there, filling a bucket. He looked up as May brought Harry near and peered at them under his wispy white eyebrows. His sight was going a little.

"Who's that pretty lass got you b'the hand, Harry?"

"It's May, Grandda'."

"Well, now . . ." he said vaguely; and muttered something to himself in that manner that was growing upon him lately. "Pretty May, is it? How are you these long days, May?"

"Well enough, Mr Hoad. Thanks for the asking. Have you done at the pump? There's a heavy job to be doing here. Best not let it settle too hard, eh Harry?"

"Funny thing," the old man said softly to Harry as May rolled up her sleeves and took hold of the pump handle. "I a'most thought she were your own mother come back. I did, then. Poor old codger, ain't I?" And he went off laughing at his own folly.

Harry could not know whether May bore any resemblance to his dead mother, Grandda' had never said anything about it before. How sadly old he was growing, all of a sudden; no longer sure of what he saw and heard. Yet the dream of a likeness to the dead woman somehow warmed and consoled Harry. What had she really been like, he wondered? Rich people, someone had told him, had their portraits painted and so for ever their features could be known. But the wives of poor farmers remained only in the memory of those who had known them; then, as those also died, all was forgotten and for ever.

Chapter Three

LUKE

Farmer Hoad had had only one child, a son. That son had made up for his own solitude by having a big family. Harry, in fact, was the last child of all – he was the tenth and had been born five years after the ninth. Once they had all lived together in the farmhouse that had stood for at least three hundred years with the forest growing up beside it, so that by now those distant downs could only be seen in winter through bare trees. The house was not large, though a good deal larger than Rangers; anyone could understand Ranger Blagden's ambition to move from one to the other. The very idea of Sam Blagden eating and sleeping where he had slept and ate filled Harry with horror.

Six sons, four daughters, two parents, one grandparent had filled Hoads Farm to overflowing. The household was a poor one, there were not enough beds to go round; the boys took turns at sleeping on the floor. All the children had been given names out of the Bible – all, that is, except Harry. His mother had died before she could choose what he should be called and his father knew a good deal less about such matters. He was not a very good farmer, either. Unlike his father, Harry's Grandda', who worked unceasingly as farmers always must, he was lazy and careless. He was forever making silly mistakes, missing his opportunities, being casual with the stock and for some reason never getting the hay cut in good time. Once his poor wife had died he saw no good reason for staying on to struggle with the farm and the forest, his huge family and his increasingly dissatisfied father. He decided to tramp the long miles to

London and seek some better fortune there.

"One less mouth," he told his family, "so one more portion for the rest."

"I'll come along wi' you, then, Dad," said Matthew, the eldest son. "That'll be two lots for 'em."

Harry was only a baby, so he was not able to remember when this happened. No one had ever spoken of it except Luke, the third son, and he only told the bare bones of the matter. There was something altogether too shocking in the business for it to be discussed – a father who walked off and left his children to get on as best they might. The fact that he was not the only local man to despair of gaining a living from that land in no way improved things. Some of those had returned with money in their pockets; but Harry's father and Matthew were never heard of again.

"You're an orphan," Sam Blagden had informed Harry.

"What's that mean?"

"No dad, no ma – you'm a nothing!" cried Sam, delighting in Harry's puzzled expression. For some years he had imagined that Sarah was his mother.

Sarah was the eldest daughter and so she took over the task of running the family. It was hard for her – a neighbour farmer's son wished to marry her, but another deserter in the family was not to be thought of. She sent him away, for the next sister was too young at that time to take on Sarah's task.

For a few years nothing further happened save growing up and working hard at farming jobs – and getting no richer, for the times in any case were hard.

Then, suddenly, the Hoad family seemed to split apart. Mark, the next brother to Matthew, married a girl from the far side of the forest and went off to live by the sea, where her two brothers were fishermen, glad to welcome a newcomer. Sometimes a message came from Mark through his wife's family – another child, and so on – but they did not come visiting. Two more sisters, Rebecca and Mary, married one year after the other and vanished into distant countryside.

Then the next brother, Elias, fell in with neighbours' sons and went off with them to Canada; he sent one scrawly letter saying they had arrived, and that was that. That left Aaron grumbling, for Elias had been his particular friend – so he went to work as gardener's boy at Stagmount Park, the estate of the Lord of the Manor, that stood grandly on rising ground to the east of the forest, showing His Lordship his lands laid out below him. Martha, the youngest girl, missed Aaron as he had missed Elias, and so she went to work in the kitchens at Stagmount. For a time she came home quite often, but then her work grew harder and her visits ceased, as did Aaron's.

In the farmhouse that had seemed so crowded there was then only Grandda', Sarah, Luke and Harry. Luke was the worker – he was the one who had the ideas and helped their grandfather in every task there was. He knew about the animals, he always recognised the best day for cutting or carrying; what he planted grew.

"Where'd we be wi'out Luke?" was a constant cry from all of them.

One day, that question had to be answered.

Even after three years, Harry could wake in terror at what had happened. Then, in the bitter-dark of his bedroom with its ceiling that sloped almost to the ground, he could not stop himself remembering. There was no pain in remembering Luke himself, the favourite brother, the almost magical companion. It was the disaster he had brought about so recklessly that made Harry bury his face in the blanket and almost wish that Luke had never happened.

"Come on out wi' me," he had said, whispering it to Harry as he shook him awake. "Come on. Never saw deer in the moonlight, did you? Never saw'm at dawn . . . Come on, then."

Harry had been back to that secret place often enough

since then, but that night was the first he knew of it - a graceful clearing among birch trees, the little river running below fast enough over the iron-streaked rocks to make a faint babble. When the moon was high the light was like no other, diffused by the fine stippling leaves of the birch, and falling, as it sometimes seemed, almost musically down to the running water . . . Though Harry had been so young at the time of that first visit, he remembered how every second had been filled - how they had crept from the house, Luke's old dog, Trumpet, at their heels, the rest silent and snuffling under the barn door because Luke had so commanded them. He remembered his bursting pride in being there with a brother so much older, so loved and admired. He recalled Luke's easy, confident manner that proclaimed the night's business to be nearing a successful conclusion.

Then Luke had gripped him by the hand to impose silence and for the first time Harry knew what he was about. Though it was a warm, soft night, Harry remembered, too, how he had shivered with fear and a terrible dread of what Luke was about to do. He saw the old dog, quivering with excitement, gazing at his master, ready and waiting for any order.

With hardly any sound, a beautiful young deer leapt up the bank and stood poised in the entry to the clearing, smelling danger, instantly alert. But even swifter, Luke struck so skilfully into the creature's throat that it fell in utter silence and lay dead.

But there was some other sound. That terrible moment when everything was changed from strange perfection to total disaster was more than merely remembered. It was carved into Harry's being by the shock of the moment, by the horror that followed.

Luke had grabbed him and breathed close to his ear - "Get home! Do's I bid. No talk. Get home. Fast!"

"What happen? Why -?"

"Quiet. Home! Home!"

24

He had given the boy a great shove that almost sent him pitching down the bank into the water.

Luke's furious urgency, his power and certainty had forced his young brother to obey him. Even so, when he heard shouts and caught the swing of a lantern, Harry had almost turned and run back to try, however feebly, to help . . . There was a shot and a terrible cry of pain from the dog. At that Harry fled home, knowing already that there was nothing anyone could do. Knowing that the forest rangers, always in conflict with poachers, had found their quarry just as surely as Luke had found his. They would not slit his throat, as Luke had slit the deer's so that it dropped soundless to the ground. But there were other penalties in wait for any convicted, as Luke must surely be, of the vile crime of stealing game from His Mighty Lordship of the Manor. Less than a year before, a forest neighbour's son had been caught poaching, hauled in front of the justices and sentenced. With many other convicted criminals he had been shipped off in chains to work for the rest of his life in Western Australia.

That was what happened to Luke. No effort on the part of Mr Kingham and his friends, members of an association formed to help prisoners, could save him. He was guilty as charged and every magistrate on the Bench had cause to keep in the good books of the Lord of the Manor.

Now at Hoads farmhouse there were only three. There were beds to spare and enough to eat. There was also a great deal more work for those who were left. Now it seemed a lifetime since Harry had started to be a farmer's boy - scaring crows, sweeping out the yard with a broom too long in the handle, chopping firewood. This was the moment when he took on the milking and the hens along with all the rest.

"Sheep must go," Grandda' had said, when they knew that Luke was never coming home. "Can't keep more'n one horse. Help wi' ploughing, then. Could be John

Tomsett'd oblige."

John Tomsett had always been a good neighbour. He was the nearest farmer to own a bull, so several of Hoads' calves had the same father. At haytime and harvest all the farmers round about helped one another, going from farm to farm as required. Old friends seen at no other time came then; hard as the work was, there was always an air of comradeship and curious contentment. Later, when the apples ripened, the Gurr brothers from the nearest village came with a great cider press, and then there were bottles stored to see the winter through.

Now that almost all the family had gone, there was a great quiet about the place. In the long summer evenings when Harry's work, so much heavier than ever before, was over and done with, he very often wondered what to do next. He roamed the forest, summer and winter, dark and light. He learnt where best to try for trout, which stream flowed into which pond, which rabbits promised best for the pot. He was a poacher in the making who would never dare ply his skills to the full – he would never poach a deer. He discovered a great deal about their ways, as much, perhaps, as Luke had known. He knew the time of year when the males sought their mates and fought for them, trampling grass and bracken into a great ring. He knew the month when the does produced their young, the mild mid-summer, and how the little creatures would follow their mothers in the more secret and silent places. Sometimes, it is true, he cast a longing glance at some young buck's meaty haunches – but though he was ready to risk fish or coney he would go no further. The deer were safe from Harry because of Luke – and because, though he might not admit it, learning their ways, watching their graceful movements and their speed had given him a fondness for the creatures, so that he would never willingly cause harm to any one of them.

"Early haying," Grandda' said, looking out over the two

fields to be cut. "See you get word round, Harry."

Spring and summer that year had been exactly right – sun by day, rain in decent proportion – so that the season was ahead of itself and would most likely stay so for the rest of the growing year.

It was a warm Sunday afternoon, just short of milking time. Grandda' was sitting on the bench against the dairy wall and Harry had sat down, too, to give him a bit of company. The old man wore a clean shirt to prove which day of the week it was, and Harry had cleaner hands than usual. Sarah had gone over the forest to the big house, hoping for a word with Aaron and Martha. She had made the trip once or twice lately and had seemed quite unexpectedly pleased to do so. "The new housekeeper's Mrs Heasman," she had told them. "Knows her way in these parts, thankfully."

For half an hour or so, Harry's precious cows had been making their way towards the milking shed, a yard or two at a time as they paused for yet one more munch. Now they stood in a row, whisking their tails and flicking their ears against the flies, peering up towards where they could hear the most important voice in their lives, Harry's, and occasionally lowering their heads and letting out a demanding moo.

"Must go," said Harry.

"You care for they beasts like childer," the old man said. He grinned, but in a way that suggested he felt the same way about Harry as did Buttercup and Rosie and the rest. He laid his hand on Harry's arm. "Never you leave home, eh Harry?"

"I wun't," said Harry, meaning it. Anxiety seemed to flow into his mind and out again. While Grandda' lived there was home – but what truly happened after? Where would home be then? This was increasingly in his mind and he could not answer his own question.

The old man looked closely at his youngest grandchild, still a delaying hand on his arm as if waiting for it to be clasped in reassurance. His manner was troubling. He had always managed the farm and everyone concerned with it with great firmness - it was strange to see the uncertainty that was shifting into his manner. Perhaps he realised suddenly what he had not thought about until now, perhaps he understood for the first time that every life has its ending. And because of that, maybe the forest had never looked so fine and fair - so many birds singing, so much leaf and blossom.

"Here's Sarah come home," Harry said, not sorry to be distracted by ordinary affairs. "It's Sarah, Grandda'. There's some feller along wi' her."

Sarah came up the yard towards them; she looked in some manner taller than usual. The man following her was no young lad but a rather fine looking fellow with broad shoulders, probably in his forties.

"Here's Mr Rolfe walked me home," Sarah said. "And this is my grandfather, Farmer Hoad, and here's my brother, Harry. Youngest of all 'us, he is."

"'do," said Grandda' and Harry.

"'do," said Mr Rolfe. "Seemed a long lonely way for the lady," he said, as if he thought he had better explain his presence.

Harry had never thought of Sarah as a 'lady', and he looked at her in astonishment, as though he must have missed something about her that Mr Rolfe had recognised.

"Sit down," Sarah said to the visitor. "I'll fetch a glass o' summat."

Mr Rolfe, it soon appeared, was His Lordship's coachman. He spoke with enthusiasm and fondness of his horses, and told how he would drive often to London and back, with his employer and his family safe inside, and a couple of footmen on the box.

"I'd soonest be in the countryside," he said. "My mother was from these parts and so I know when I'm come home. She was an Eede."

There was much exclaiming over this, for the very first

cowman employed at Hoads had been called Eede.

By this time the cows were losing patience. Rosie, Clover and Harry's favourite, Buttercup, kept up a continual lowing. Dainty and Heather were resting but would soon be taken for mating with Tomsett's bull. Even five cows meant a lot of planning and remembering. Harry went off to his charges with the least bit less willingness than was usual. He talked to them, of course, as he worked his way from one stall to the next, and the swish of the milk into the pail sounded its usual almost musical note. But Harry's mind was more than half on the grown-ups and what they might be talking about by now.

The job was done and Harry was carrying the first pail to be tipped into the churn, when he saw Sarah waving Mr Rolfe on his way. The visitor swept off his hat and raised it high as he smiled a farewell. They would see him again, that was clear enough. Not quite admitting it, Harry felt a curious gloom settle from nowhere on his busy imagination. He knew something important was happening but could not decide if he would like what it might be.

Chapter Four

HAY-TIME

His Lordship of the Manor's coachman, Mr Rolfe - his first name, Sarah told them, was Ben - did indeed come visiting frequently. Soon it became clear that he came whenever time allowed. Harry and Grandda' watched and wondered. At last each knew so well what the other was thinking that one of them was bound to speak of the business.

"Is he come courting, Grandda'?"

"What else, I'd say?"

"Shall she have'm?"

"Deserves a good husband, eh Harry? Think what she done for us, all the long years. And he tell once he had a wife died young and left no son nor daughter. Ask me, that's a lonely chap needs a mite of comfort."

Harry was silent for a bit, but his thoughts were so gloomy he was bound to put them into words.

"How'd ever we do wi'out Sarah?"

"Have to manage. What c'd you cook us for dinner, Harry?"

Harry knew he could manage a rabbit stew, for Luke had shown him when once they made a fire out on the forest.

"I'd do better," his grandfather told him. "I can bake a hedgehog. Cover it in thick clay, see, and put 'un in a fire. When the clay's cracked off, the spines come wi'it. Had that of a gypsy woman, one St Giles's market. That's the tastiest thing ever, that is."

They were both silent, considering glumly, baked hedgehog or no, a life in which they must make their own meals - like the two farming brothers at Fleet Farm, just short of the village; as miserable a pair as you could look for.

In fact, like all the rest, ten days or so later, the brothers came to give a hand with Hoads' haying. Harry wondered if he should ask them about baked hedgehog, but could not quite bring himself to it. The first cutting ushered in a spell of hard work for everyone – and when their own hay was in, Harry and Sarah would be off to help at other farms round about. The weather had been so good that the crop was as big as any they could remember, the grass so high and lush that it fell with what seemed like a contented sigh into its long scythed rows. How long, Harry wondered, before he was tall enough and strong enough in the shoulders to handle a scythe? There was plenty for him to do without it, but the fine, rhythmic movement was almost like a special sort of music which he longed to be able to make for himself. Not that he thought of it quite like that, perhaps.

The weather stayed as everyone wished it to stay, dry, not too hot, nor too cold at night to dampen the day's cutting or turning or raking. By the time the sun went in, with thunder rumbling through a wicked sky, they had moved on to the final stage of rick building. That was when Harry worked hardest.

May had come with the rest to work at the haying in Hoads' fields, dragging Sam along with her. He seldom did more than kick the hay about and throw stones at fleeing rabbits – which had made Harry even more determined to work as hard as any one of the grown men.

"Go easy a bit, Harry," May said. "You do Luke's work as well as your own." And when he did not answer, but went red, she said softly – "Did he ever tell we were to marry one day?"

"He never tell. But I did see it plain."

"Well, then – say I'm your sister that tell you not to work yourself over weary."

34

Over weary was a gentle way of describing Harry's state at the end of each haymaking day. He had his own work to get through as well – the cows and the hens, the business of carting up to the dairy whatever milk Sarah needed for butter and cream; and humping the rest, along with the day's eggs, to the shelter by the gate. Old Sloper Scriven came every day with his horse and cart, to supply his own dairy and those neighbours in need. What with one thing and another, there were many nights through the haying season when Harry fell into bed in his clothes and had to be shaken awake each morning.

Then it was the last day, with the rick thatched and standing neat as a toy in the corner of the home field. Though this part of the farm year could not rate as high as the harvest that lay ahead, which would call for a fine supper when it was done, the haymakers at Hoads Farm sat down in the barn and drank great draughts of beer and cider in celebration of a job well done.

Sam Blagden scorned the merriment. He hung on the field gate by the rick and broke into one of his favourite rhyming taunts –

"Farmer Harry, Farmer Harry, cut the hay that others carry!"

"You get off home, you!" Harry yelled back.

"This here'll be my home one day soon, see if it en't."

"Talk sense, can't you?"

"The old man'll be dead soon. Any knows it. Think you can farm on your own, do you? No fear! None'd see that. It's the orphanage for you, Harry Hoad."

"Shut your gob and get away from here!"

"Farmer Harry, Farmer Harry . . ." Sam shouted over his shoulder as he ran off.

Harry watched him go. The orphanage! What was that lout talking about? A lad with so many brothers and sisters need never lack a home. Need he? Then he thought how Sarah would surely marry Ben Rolfe and go off to live in the coachman's cottage at Stagmount; how Matthew had long vanished and Mark gone to a different life. Rebecca and Mary had not been heard of for well over a year, Elias was in a far part of the world as Luke was, while Martha and Aaron had no home but the servants' attics at their place of work.

As he turned back to the house, Harry saw his grandfather thanking the neighbours for their help and wishing them well with what came next. Sarah was beside him, and Ben Rolfe. Ben was not so very tall, but Grandda' did indeed look small and shaky beside him.

On the Sunday after haymaking was done with, Grandda' sat on the bench outside the kitchen door. He and the old sheepdog, Fury, stretched out nearby, dozed in the mild afternoon sunshine. Ben Rolfe had had dinner with them and when it was over, he and Sarah had gone off to walk in the forest – and no doubt to take a step nearer to whatever plans they might be considering. Ben would perhaps be wondering if the time was now right for him to ask Sarah to marry him; Sarah probably feeling that he was taking far too long about it. Harry had meant to go that afternoon to one of his secret fishing places, but he knew Sarah would be angry if he went off leaving their grandfather on his own – in case something happened. Harry did not know precisely what was meant by 'something' but he knew he must stay.

He wandered about, kicking at stones, wondering which way Ben and Sarah had chosen, and where would be a good place to pause – perhaps to look at some distant spire and argue which church it belonged to, since neither had ever noticed it from that point before. Then Harry imagined them on the little bridge below the mill stream, where Sarah would be able to lean on the birchwood rail. There was no view whatsoever from there, so why should they pause? Well, there they would be, Harry decided, grinning as he made himself this graceful picture, Sarah would lean on the rail and gaze down at the water

and Ben would then put his arm across her shoulders . . .
Nothing in life would be the same again, Harry decided.
It would just have to be baked hedgehog for dinner.

Harry could hardly fail to dread the thought of Sarah's
leaving home, however matter-of-fact she had always
seemed towards him. Already, since she had met Ben, her
manner had softened. She was losing that sharp edge to
her voice and when she had children of her own, Harry
knew she would not only love them, she would let them
be sure she did so. She had, of course, never been down-
right unkind to Harry, had always cared for him in every
way needed – but she had never made him feel she loved
him as a sister should. She had, he decided very wisely,
done her duty without ever suggesting that she enjoyed
it. He knew, for Luke had told him, that she had given up
her first chance of marriage in order to look after the
family. She deserved her happiness with this new
admirer.

So much contemplating and considering had taken
Harry, kicking a stone ahead of him, down to the track
that passed the entrance to the farmyard. He remembered
he had not picked up the money old Sloper paid out at the
end of each week's collection of milk and eggs. It was left
in a cup without a handle behind a clump of dock by the
gatepost.

As Harry bent down to pick up the cup, old Fury
roused himself from his place by Grandda'. He came
down to Harry, barking without much energy but doing
the job he had been so long accustomed to. No other dog
troubled to join in. Harry looked up, expecting Sarah and
Ben Rolfe. But it was a man on horseback who was
approaching. There were seldom many riding about the
forest that Harry did not know, and he knew them first
by their horses. This was an unfamiliar, rather too sturdy
grey.

But he knew the rider well. The rider was Mr
Kingham.

"Well, Harry – and how do you do?" Mr Kingham dismounted and hitched his rein to the gatepost. "A busy time of year and the best of weather for it."

"We bin haying, master."

"And soon it shall be harvest. The land is a hard master, Harry. Nothing for it but to stick to the calendar." He smiled his rather too grave smile. "You will wonder why I am here."

"Yes, sir. I do wonder."

"Is your grandfather at home? Or your sister?"

"My sister's out. Grandda's up b'the kitchen door."

Harry tried not to frown or look puzzled, since Mr Kingham was always so calm himself. He never gave the least idea of what he was about, just going his way in a quiet and steady manner that was both admirable and exasperating.

"Then I'll speak to your grandfather, Harry, if you will allow me."

Harry went ahead of him. The old man was still dozing. Harry touched his shoulder.

"Grandda' – someone come to see you. It's Mr Kingham." And he repeated, "Mr Kingham's here," in a voice that suggested he could not quite believe it. "Mr Kingham, Grandda'," he said yet again, and then the old man grunted, opened his eyes and stared round him.

"Good afternoon to you, Mr Hoad," said the visitor. "No – stay seated, I beg you, for I shall like to sit beside you. This is a fine outlook across the forest."

"What's amiss, sir? Has young Harry done that he oughtn't?"

"No, no. It is another grandson of yours I am concerned with. I have news, through friends from those distant parts, of your grandson, Luke."

The old man peered at the visitor, cocking his head slightly, as if he thought he might not have heard correctly. He turned to Harry and muttered, as if to him alone, "What's that he say? Luke? Did 'un say Luke?"

"Aye, he did, he did!"

"You know well," Mr Kingham was saying, "that I and my wife are concerned with a church body that cares for prisoners. We have dear friends who work in such places as convicted men are sent to. Do you recall, Mr Hoad?"

"I do. Indeed I do! Should I forget, then, what you spoke out for Luke, those dreadful times?"

"Some such unhappy men do not survive the terrible journey. But I am here to tell you that your grandson was more fortunate. He is alive and is in Western Australia. My friends have written to tell me of this. Poor lad, he may be leading a life of terrible deprivation – far, far beyond what he could deserve. But he is alive – and we shall see that the best is done for him."

"Never come back home, though – never. Eh, sir?"

"I think not, Mr Hoad. But we shall contrive him a good master. Believe me, Luke shall be settled with a farmer and take up the business he knows best."

"But never, ever home . . . ?" Harry said.

"That is an empty part of the world, Harry. Men are needed and this is one way to find them." Mr Kingham smiled, then, and rose. "There. I have brought you some sort of good news – haven't I, Harry?"

"Yes, master."

"No better greeting ever," his grandfather said.

Harry went with Mr Kingham to his tethered horse and held the bridle while he mounted. How firm he sat, without pretence of grace but steady as any rock. He waved a farewell as he moved off, then wheeled and came near.

"There may be other news before long, Harry," he said, rather solemnly. "Now – take care of that poor old man. God bless you."

This time he moved away firmly and soon had vanished in among the crowding trees that bordered the track carrying him home.

Chapter Five

NEWS

In the hottest days of summer when every farmer was watching the sky as harvest time drew near, Harry looked solemnly round his herd of five. He did indeed feel he could by now call it his, though Sarah still took care of the calves when they were born. Even five cows need careful managing; young as he was, Harry could claim to know what he was up to. At present he had only three to milk - Buttercup, Rosie and Dainty. Once Heather and Clover produced their calves there would again be plenty of milk for Sloper Scriven to collect each day, and better money in the cup at the gate. The last three calves that Harry's cows had produced had gone to Farmer Tomsett; he was building up his herd after a winter in which sickness had greatly damaged his stock - anyway, the bull who had fathered them was of course his bull. Harry wished that the next two calves might stay at Hoads to replace the two oldest members; they were past their prime and gave less milk than paid for their keep. He knew their time had come. They must go.

"Must, must," he muttered, as he tried to plan in a true farmerly manner, without any nonsense.

This was the first time since he took over the care of the cows and their milking that Harry had found himself thinking so sternly. He hated it. Buttercup was the oldest of the five and Buttercup he dearly loved. Sometimes when he had longed to be comforted for a hard life, for rising in the dark cold winter mornings and trudging through frost and snow to the yard, he had pushed his face against her warm flank and cried lonely tears. And now what he had to admit was the fact that when those two older cows were sold, it would almost certainly be for meat.

Harry knew very well that farming was a stern business, much concerned with life and death of one sort and another. It could never be all pretty long-lashed calves and fluffy chicks but he was young enough to wish it could be so. Perhaps Buttercup and Heather might even now find a purchaser ready to keep them as they were for a time.

Harry stood by the field gate, the sun on the back of his neck, solemnly chewing at a long blade of grass – just like any old farmer ten times his age. There was a stillness in the air, a silent drowsiness, as though the season hung on the brink of some fulfilment. And so it did – for this was the moment when the farming year moved to its true meaning; when the care and labour of months past would be tied into the triumphant sheaves of harvest time. Then farmers everywhere might see with satisfaction the gathering in of a year's hard toil. It might not always be as bountiful as they had hoped, yet it was at least a pause, brief enough, in that round of labour which claimed some part of every minute of every day.

Down in the yard there was a sudden outbreak of barking. Harry could see a corner of the house, where the dairy was, and through its open door he could just see Sarah working. Below the house, where the yard melted into the forest track, he saw Sam Blagden. He was riding his pony in wild circles among the hens, so that their comfortable scratching and pecking had become clucking and screeching as they scattered in every direction. To add to the noise, the dogs had joined in and were snapping and barking hysterically at the pony's heels.

Sometimes Sam made Harry feel half his age and size, sometimes twice, three, four times his age and size – and that was how he felt now. He spat out the blade of grass, wiped his hands on his dirty smock, and moved off down the slope to the yard.

"Hey, you!" he shouted. It was less of a bellow than he had planned, so he tried again. "Hey! You! Sam Blagden!"

Sam glanced up, made some rude reply, then continued his antics.

"Stop that, will you? Leave they hens be! Get out my yard."

Sam pulled up and gave his hard taunting laugh.

"Yourn, is it?"

"Get out o' here." Harry glared. "Why'n't you in school? Playing truant, eh?"

"School's over. I come a' purpose to tell."

It was still July. Holidays had never started until August – in time for everyone to help with the harvest.

"What's that mean – school's over?"

"What it say, what else? Mr Kingham said to tell you. He wun't be there n'more. There'll be another master. So my dad tell I'll not need to go."

Harry felt as though his breath might leave him altogether. Another master . . . ? Why?

"What come to Mr Kingham, then?"

"How'd I know?" Sam began riding in circles round and round Harry, making the dogs wilder than ever. "New master next time, that's what. Tell any as were'n't in school that day. Tell Harry Hoad. Call you b'name, he did. Teacher's pet!"

"Where'll he be, then? Mr Kingham. Where'll he be?" Harry thought of Luke, of Mr Kingham's promises. "He'd never just go away. He never would."

"Boo hoo, what'll we do?" shouted Sam, wheeling the pony at last and trotting out of the yard. "He'll not likely tarry for Hoady old Harry!"

Screeching with laughter, he kicked the pony into a hard canter and turned for home.

Harry hardly knew Sam had gone. He had come down to the yard one person – Harry Hoad with a friend called

Mr Kingham who seemed the wisest and the kindest and the most honourable man in the world – and now he stood, it seemed to him, without that friend. It was as if everything had been taken away – help for Luke, kindness to Grandda', a teacher so patient he was ready to welcome a pupil able to appear in school less than once in any month . . . What would happen now? Would he never go to school again? Would any other teacher put up with him? He was only halfway to reading and writing – was that as far as he was ever to get? Harry was so struck by wretchedness and disappointment that he dropped down on one knee among the still fussing hens and put his hands over his face.

Sarah saw him from the dairy. She came hurrying, wiping her hands on her apron as she came.

"Harry! What come about? What'd that beastly Sam do to you? You're crying! Crying – a great lad like you!"

He shrugged her away as she pulled him to his feet.

"Leave off, will you? Sam bring me bad news, that's what."

"What, then? What bad news?"

"I shan't tell. I wun't speak it. Leave me be, do."

His voice had risen, he was shouting. Not only Sarah but the two dogs became more and more confused. He felt Sarah grabbing his arms, trying to turn him towards her, but he fought her off. Then she had him by the shoulders and was shaking him.

"Listen! Listen, do! I'm your own sister, en't I? Tell me, Harry. Tell me, do."

For the first time, Harry was still. He looked at her and then away. She had never before used quite that soothing voice, as if she were truly sorry for him and wanted to make things better. He knew she had changed a lot lately, and knew it was because she was in love with Ben Rolfe and happier than she had been for many years. She was his sister, Sarah, just as she had reminded him, and almost without warning she was the sister he had always missed and needed, even though he had hardly known it.

He stopped struggling and leant against her, shoving his face into her shoulder - almost as if she were his favourite, Buttercup.

"Now tell," she said. "Tell."

By the time Harry had finished his miserable tale, his tears had started all over again. His face was wet and he was hiccuping like some sad four-year-old.

"What'll I tell Grandda'? There was all that about Luke . . . What's to happen now? How'll Grandda' think when he hear it?"

"Ask me, it's best not to tell," Sarah said, frowning. "Let be for a while. Anyways - who's to tell if Sam spoke true? He's a lying mawkin often enough."

"Mr Kingham said to tell me - he said to Sam, 'Tell Harry Hoad.' "

"There's a mistake, surelye. He never could've said what Sam tell he say. Now - give over do, Harry, or you'll not see out your eyes ever again."

Her voice had sharpened, yet still it was a new voice and he did his best to obey it. He rubbed his hands across his face, leaving dismal smears behind.

"You never did want me a scholar," he said. "Got your way now, all right."

"Hush, do. I said a lot I never rightly meant. Things've turned different. I'll tell you now and not speak it again till times change - Ben and me shall get married one day. But don't you ever think I'll go off and leave Grandda' and you. I never will. Don't breathe a word o' that, if you please, or I'll never do a good thing for you any time."

Because she was speaking to him so firmly and so differently, Harry could not say what he wanted to. Such a promise could comfort him in a way - but it could not stop his need to ask what would happen when Grandda' died. For that was surely the 'one day' when she and Ben would get wed. All that would be left of the farm household, all that would be left of a family of ten brothers and sisters would be the youngest. He could not stay there alone – and if he was not to be there, where would he be?

Chapter Six

ANOTHER MASTER

The day after Sam's visit his sister, May, came calling. She found Sarah and Harry by the potato patch. Harry was digging the potatoes and Sarah was counting them into small sacks. There were five rows to be worked over today, all neatly earthed-up and weedless; another six rows were later-planted, they would not be ready for a good while yet.

The moment she saw May, Sarah broke out into the story of Sam's behaviour, though she kindly left out the part about Harry's distress.

"He's a wicked young devil," May said. "I never do know when to believe'm. My mother brought me up proper, but his was n'more'n a wild gypsy and it come out in Sam. My dad should've known better'n to marry her."

"Well, she's dead, poor thing," said Sarah, "and need never know the way he's gone."

"That's so," agreed May. She flicked a slightly mocking glance at Sarah. "And I doubt I ever heard you speak so soft before, Sarah Hoad. Whatever could've come to you, I wonder?"

"Never you mind," said Sarah, refusing to rise to this faint, good-natured mockery. "Anyways, it's a bit soft letting Harry to school. He'll never need book learning, any more'n his grandfather."

By that time, work on the potatoes had come to an end. The two young women walked side by side to the house, with Harry behind them carrying a supply for the kitchen. The discussion about what Mr Kingham had said or not said continued to occupy them. He never would have said what Sam said he said, came from May; if he did, Sam could've been a sight more decent about it, from Sarah. Harry stayed silent. It would have been difficult to get a word in, anyway; but what kept him so silent was the extreme wretchedness that had settled on him since yesterday. He could not imagine how it would ever have an end.

"Whatever he did say," May decided, as they went into the kitchen, "it got to be found out, once for all."

"How?"

"I'll go to town and ask, o'course. Harry'd best come along wi' me."

"Harry's busy."

"We'll go mid-morning. He'll be back for milking."

At that Harry joined in. "Will I wear a clean shirt?"

"Yes, if you've got it."

"If he has, that's my doing," grumbled Sarah. She began to sound more like the Sarah they had known for so long. "Go, then – go if you must. You'll miss your dinner."

May laughed at Harry's face. "I'll bring along summat for both us, Harry – don't you fret. Tomorrer. Mid-morning. See you be ready on time."

The next day, when May and Harry set out, it was very hot. They might have gone quicker by the old track that quit the forest very soon and led between hedges and fields. Cutting across the forest was cooler, for there was a great deal of birch to give them shade, and one stretch that took them through a beech wood that was not only cool but almost dark. It was a place much frequented by deer and they had left their mark – many tree trunks were robbed of bark where the males had rubbed their antlers. The soft velvet that coated them when they were newly grown, itched and teased and had to be got rid of. It was the time of year when the does had had their fawns – called the *fence month*, from older times when they were protected by the law of the forest from all other animals. There was no grazing during the fence month, no cutting of bracken, no cutting of wood. Nearly all the land on the edges of the forest, and further, had such rights attached - *right of common*, it was called, and it was so old that no king and no lord of any manor had been able to take it away. Mr Kingham had once spoken of such matters at school and Harry had rushed home to tell his grandfather. "Any know that," was all he got in reply.

There were deer moving today about the beech wood. The fawns lay often alone while their mothers foraged for food. May and Harry were too used to such things to take much notice, though May did pause to look at one of the little creatures as it lay asleep with its head neatly tucked against its haunch.

Any sight or talk of the deer was bound to remind Harry of Luke, and it was Luke they talked about as they went on their way through the hot summer noon.

"Mr Kingham said Luke'd be helped some way. He never would've said it and then gone away."

Harry spoke for May's comfort as well as his own. What he did not speak of was what he had remembered after going to his bed last night - how Mr Kingham had said something about 'other news'. He had come back on purpose to say it - 'There may be other news before long', or some such matter. Was that news to have been *No more school?*

When they came to the town, there was the school - perhaps Harry had half expected that it would have vanished. The gates were chained; there was no sign of anyone living in the schoolhouse; the curtains were down.

"Ask at the parsonage," May decided. "It's the church people runs the school. They'll know what come to Mr and Mrs Kingham."

They passed the church as the clock struck two. The house they were looking for was placed at right angles to the churchyard wall. It was a flat, neat-faced house, with a well-shone brass step to its grey painted front door.

Shining just as brightly as the step were the knocker, the bell-pull, the letter-box and a brass plate with the name of the place – not The Parsonage, but *The Rectory*. What was the difference? Harry wanted to know. But May had not the least idea, contenting herself with giving the bell a tug. They heard the ringing echo inside the house; then silence; then footsteps. The door was opened by a very small woman in a cap and apron too big for her. She frowned.

"Other door," she said – and closed the front door instantly.

For a second May looked as if she might turn and run away, but Harry had already seen the side door sign at the end of the wall. *Tradesmen*, it said.

The side door was opened by the same woman.

"Yes?"

"Is the parson at home, if you please?" asked May.

"You mean the Rector. Who wants him?"

"Well, please, we do."

"And who are you?"

Harry noticed that May stopped being frightened and tossed her head a bit as she replied. "I am Miss May Blagden," she said, in a voice she had most surely never used before in her life. "And this is Master Harry Hoad, Farmer Hoad's son. We have summat – something – to speak about."

"Fancy that," said the servant. "Come in and wait there. I'll see what Mr Goodhew thinks about this. He's home, but that don't prove nothing."

"Say we come about the school," said May.

There was no reply. The woman went off along the passage towards a wide hall. They heard her knock at a door out of sight but they could not hear what she said when she was called to go in. May and Harry dared not look at one another until she reappeared.

"Come on, then, if you must," she called. "And don't keep the master too long. He's better things to do."

At that May grabbed Harry by the elbow and they went fast to where the door was being held open.

"Them, sir," said his servant; and banged the door behind them.

Harry had never before been inside any house save farmhouses and cottages – and once the schoolhouse. He looked around him almost furtively, as though here was something he should not really be seeing – the heavy dark curtains, the bookshelves floor to ceiling, the chairs with padded leather seats. A rich wallpaper, gilt on dark green, was something he could not even have imagined; nor yet the handsome huge desk at which sat the Rector, Mr Goodhew. He was a biggish man with amazingly black hair, thick and hard-brushed so that it sat on his head like a cap. He waved his hand in the direction of the visitors as if suggesting that the work on which he was engaged was too important to be interrupted; nor did he know how long it would take.

"You may be seated," he said, without looking up.

There were two high-backed chairs side by side. May and Harry sat down gingerly. To have exchanged glances would have seemed like shouting, so utterly quiet was the room – though Mr Goodhew's pen did scratch a little. It was a good seven or eight minutes before he reached some conclusion or other, when he laid down his pen, leant back in his chair and gave them his attention.

"Well?"

May answered, her voice rather low and a little hoarse.

"We come about the school, sir."

"The school? Yes? Yes? What about the school?"

"My brother got told by the master – "

Mr Goodhew broke in. "Is this your brother? Then can't he speak for himself?"

"No, sir. My brother's Sam Blagden."

"Then why is he not come?"

"Because this is Harry Hoad, sir," said May, sounding by now rather fussed. "It's him'd wish to know was this true."

"And why should it not be?"

May blinked at his sharp tone but managed to answer. "It did seem justly it'd be a mistake."

"The master did not make himself clear," said Mr Goodhew, tapping impatiently on the desk top with his long pale fingers. "It is he – the master himself – who chooses to leave the school, not the school to be rid of him. But there are, of course, others well qualified to take over. We shall not see Mr Kingham at the school again – by his own choice – but I shall myself be in charge until the parish appoints another."

Looking across the desk top at him, Harry wondered if this should be called good news or bad. May decided it must be good, if only for Harry's sake. She smiled quite cheerfully.

"Then Harry here may come like he always done."

"As he always did . . ." Mr Goodhew almost smiled. "So this country lad is fearful that he may not get to school. That is indeed praiseworthy. Good fellow. Good fellow."

"Only I never do get to school more'n about twice in a season," Harry began.

He was cut short. "Twice in a season? What's that? What's that? I fear, my young friend, that school's not for you – it is for industrious lads. No pupil was ever allowed a desk who comes to use it but twice in any season. I fear you are here only to waste my time. Let's have no more of such nonsense."

With that he picked up a small silver handbell that stood beside the ink-stand, and rang it vigorously.

"Good day to you," he said, returning to his work. "Polly shall show you out."

They were out of the room, down the passage, into the street before they knew it. The door shut hard behind them.

Even though they had been kept waiting, the day's business was over in half the time they had expected. Now came the long walk home with matters very little clearer than they had been when they set out. Certainly they knew now that the school was at present closed. It was very clear that Mr Kingham was out of favour at the Rectory. It was likely, May thought, that someone had told him, if he wanted to go, then to go at once – which explained the early summer closing. But they had not discovered anything at all to explain the situation fully.

"Maybe he took sick," said Harry, as they went rather slowly through the hot afternoon.

"Much good that'd do any'us."

"Maybe the parson just like to be a teacher."

"Taught us, didn' he!" cried May, laughing a bit.

They grew very hot as they walked and presently they sat down by a clump of fir trees on a high point which showed the forest shimmering in the heat. Nothing stirred to break the stillness nor the silence. Empty of bird flight, the sky had had its colour drained by the sun, so that it hung over all like some bleached coverlet.

"Once I come here wi' Luke," May said. "Know what, Harry? That were the day he kissed me first time ever." She looked sideways at him. "Are you laughing?"

He shook his head. There was little to laugh over when it came to Luke.

"Wish I could be a great bird and fly across the world to him. I do. I'll never wed any other, that's flat. I'll live lonely all my life."

They sat side by side on a fallen trunk and thought about Luke – and if the terrible business remained for Harry the worst thing in his life, he knew that for May it was worse than the worst. He wished he could tell her he knew that, but it was too difficult. Instead, pretending he had not noticed she was crying by now, he got up and stretched and said they'd better be on their way or Sarah would have something to say. He strode off ahead of her, as if he were some other Luke, with the wisdom and skills of more years than he could claim.

He shouted – "Race you home!"

But leaving the shade of the trees, May only followed him slowly. As they sat there, the sun had suddenly lost some of its afternoon power and now a gentler air helped them homewards. Harry kept stopping and looking back, but May did not attempt to catch him up. She walked with her head down, sometimes kicking at the dry and sandy ground as if she must strike at something.

Harry waited for her when he came to Rangers, but they parted with no more words. The purpose of the visit and its sorry failure had been pushed aside because they had named Luke, who had been the most important thing in both their lives.

Chapter Seven

HARVEST HOME

The best of any harvest will almost certainly be the harvest supper. Even if the weather has been unkind, the harvest less than hoped for and the future therefore troubled, a harvest supper sets all that aside; it seals the farmer's year.

At Hoads, since the household was a small one, more help was needed than at any other of the forest farms. Everyone had turned up to give a hand, several without being asked. Therefore Sarah was determined to provide a supper she could be proud of. Twenty-two persons sat down in the barn, the long trestle table left over from better times almost bending with the weight of the food she had managed to assemble, helped out by neighbourly contributions. May had worked with Sarah all day to get the meal ready. She baked bread at home while Sarah boiled the great ham that had been smoking in the chimney corner for months. Then there was pigeon pie in the largest dish to be found, potatoes in their jackets, lettuce and radishes and beetroot, hard-boiled eggs and tomatoes. There was apple tart, jam tart, custard tart, marmalade tart. There were jellies red, jellies yellow, jellies green. Ginger bread jostled ginger biscuits. There was ale, there was cider, there was lemonade, there was ginger beer. There was so much to arrange that May and Sarah only just finished the job in time to wash and change into clean dresses before the first guests turned in off the forest.

Because Ranger Blagden had lent a hand with rick building, at hay and at harvest, he, too, was at the supper. That meant one unwelcome guest – two, if you counted Sam. Probably only Harry was much bothered by Sam that evening. Anyway, it was a grown-up occasion at which the younger sort were of small importance – most of them would have fallen asleep before the evening was over. As for Sam, he was too busy helping himself to food to find much time for silly behaviour. The fact that his father was there had very little to do with slightly improved manners – Sam could do as he liked and his father would only laugh comfortably.

Various of the women who had added their gifts to the table helped Sarah and May as they rushed about making sure that everyone was happy; as they refilled glasses and took away dirty dishes, as they pressed one guest after another to second helpings, third helpings, unnumbered helpings.

The guests had entered in good time, exchanged greetings, chosen their places – all in quiet good humour and without jostling or loud voices. But by the time the ham was down to its bone, the pies and other meats demolished, the greenstuff all cleared and the puddings on their way, the noise was increasing by the second. Along with all the rest, not only the pies and meat but the apples and the fruit cake and the biscuits, a great deal of beer and cider had vanished, too. Voices grew louder, demanding attention as jokes began to be told to increasingly rough bellows of laughter – and then re-told to even louder roars because only half the table had been able to hear what was said the first time. The women looked at one another and raised their eyebrows, and some of the children were sent outside into the innocent evening air. Harry glanced often at his grandfather, who sat in his rightful place, at the head of the table. At the bottom end, since he was without any possible question the man of highest authority present, the representative of the Lord of the Manor, sat Ranger Blagden. From his lofty manner it might have been thought that he was the Lord himself . . .

Now the eating really was over – the drinking would

certainly continue. There were a few biscuits left on one plate, a single slice of gingerbread on another. Some plain bread remained, but little more than crusts, while the huge fruit cake brought by Widow Sawkins – she had her eye, it was said, on Ranger Blagden – was nothing now but a remnant of crumbs and currants, almonds and cherries. Harry saw that Sam was moving around and quietly mopping up such remains, so he seized the cake crumbs, the biscuits, the crusts and the one slice of gingerbread and took them outside to the dogs; they had been waiting hopefully ever since the food was first carried into the barn.

As he stopped and spoke softly to the dogs, Harry saw the first strange glow of the rising moon. It was not quite full, but good enough to celebrate any ordinary farmer's harvest – no doubt it would be in better shape when the manor harvest was carried. Harry stood watching as the glow became a line of light which took shape as the rim of a huge dish that would soon slide fully into view. He waited until half of it had appeared, the colour of a pumpkin at that moment, but soon, as it grew bigger and rounder, changing to a huge golden sovereign. It was hard to believe that in a few hours' time it would be riding high, neither pumpkin nor sovereign, but a silver platter throwing light and shadow over the whole of the forest.

Behind Harry there came a lot more shouting and laughter, as the girls cleared the table of dirty dishes and carried them away to the pump, while the men began to shift benches and the long table out of the way to make room for the dancing that would follow. There was a loud cry:

"The moon! The moon's up!"

One or two came to the barn door, but since the big end door stood open, most of them could see the moon from where they were.

As if in welcome, the ale, the cider was raised in mugs

and tumblers whose work was not nearly over.

"Here's to harvest! Here's to next year's!"

Then from inside the barn came the first notes of Johnny Turner's concertina, the first scrape from Arthur Wood's old fiddle. That brought forth the loudest cries of all, for Arthur was ninety-one in a week's time and he had played at every harvest home since he was a lad of fifteen. It was as if the party had barely begun until now, when it blossomed at once into a merriment that would last till midnight. But not a moment longer. At twelve o'clock goodbyes would be said – for this was a Saturday evening and Sunday was no day for riotous behaviour.

Now the music was really speeding up. The sound of the feet sliding on an earth floor beaten hard by a hundred or more years of hard usage became part of the beat itself, and clapping hands increased the rhythm. Mostly these were old country dances performed to country tunes like *Oh, Good Ale* and *Sportsmen Arouse*, like *Pretty Polly Perkins*, from a different place altogether – she was a London girl – and noisiest of all *Here's a Health unto His Majesty*, its *fa-las* fairly shaking the rafters. Those who were not dancing sang the songs, for the dancers performed with such vigour they had little breath left. It was the older women, sitting round the edges of activity, who not only sang with great gusto but also looked after the smallest children – and still found time for a bit of gossip and some nudging when any one pair danced together more than twice. And no doubt many a romance was started that night as at any other harvest supper.

Sadly for Sarah, Ben Rolfe had had to drive His Lordship and family to London that week, and no one knew when they might return. But Sarah was happy enough knowing that Ben would much rather be there than in London. She had never made a better hostess, though she danced once or twice between talking to the guests, seeing to their needs and calling up one of the other helpers when she saw any empty glass. Harry thought that the drink must be running out by now.

For him, as for Sam and the other children, the party itself was gradually slowing down. The younger ones ran and skipped outside in the moonlight, but even that ended as they grew weary at being up and about so late. Many slipped back inside to sit by their mothers, even to fall asleep as they settled on the floor beside them and leant against a convenient knee.

Sam was not tired.

"Any food indoor?" he asked Harry. "Hungry."

"Stay it, then. You ate plenty enough for ten. I saw! Food don't grow on trees – "

"Apples does."

"Clever Dick."

"Pears does. Plums does. Any food I'd want to see is growing on a bush or tree."

"Eggs ain't."

"Eggs'd do fine! Come on'n find 'em."

Harry wondered whether to hit him or just walk away. He knew May would hate it if they started fighting again, so he walked away. That meant Sam set up his usual taunting. But it only lasted a few seconds, for a horseman rode into the yard and Harry immediately had something better to do than fuss about Sam Blagden. The rider was Ben Rolfe, and Harry dashed to greet him.

"Ben! You got here! What come to you?"

"Took the road s'mornin' in bright sun. Ended in bright moon. Just in time, am I? Hope so."

Harry ran ahead of him into the barn. As it happened the music had just stopped and the dancers were standing back, the men mopping at their faces, the girls fanning themselves with limp hands, pushing the hair back from their foreheads.

"Sarah!" yelled Harry. "He's here!"

He shouted into a sudden silence that might have been specially planned. It broke into a roar as one of them pushed Sarah forward and another pulled Ben into the barn towards her. Sarah was instantly scarlet, while Ben looked so sheepish that there came a great yell of laughter.

The noise died as Ben straightened his shoulders and with a curiously unexpected dignity held out his hand to Sarah, drawing her to his side. He put his arm round her. Everyone fell totally silent, listening, smiling and nodding with pleasure at what they were fairly certain Ben was going to say.

In the quiet Ben's voice sounded at once strong and gentle.

"The right moment for a bit of news," he said. "Sarah tell me two days past she's willing we get wed."

There was a greater roar then than there had been all through that noisy evening. They crowded round, the men slapping Ben on the back, shaking his hand; the women patting and kissing Sarah – who looked to Harry a completely different, almost unknown person. Then Johnny and Arthur played a long chord and went vigorously into *A Jolly Good Fellow*.

After that there seemed, somehow, nothing more that could happen and the party began from that moment to break up gently. With many cries of delight and thanks and promises for next time, they moved gradually from the barn out into the moonlight.

While Ben spoke and the whole gathering rose to an exciting moment, Harry had looked over at Grandda' and then begun pushing his way towards him. Before he was near enough to speak he saw that Sarah, too, was on her way towards the old man. She reached him just as Harry did, and bent down beside him.

"It'll be all right, Grandda'," Harry heard her say. "Ben's a patient man. He'll not take me away – not while I'm needed here, surelye."

Their grandfather said something that Harry did not hear. He patted Sarah's hand and smiled up at her. But he looked a bit dazed, Harry thought.

"See you indoors, Grandda'," Sarah was saying. "It's

late. You'll be needing your bed." And she helped him up.

They went together, very slowly, down from the barn to the farmhouse and vanished inside.

Harry stayed long enough to see the last guest out of the yard on to one or other of several homeward ways. Now indeed the moon was so high that all in sight was brilliantly illuminated – high trees, low trees, the trickling stream, the distant downs. In twos and threes and fours, fathers with sleeping children in their arms, mothers following, some yawning as they went, boys and girls arm in arm, new lovers hand in hand, they vanished gradually one way or another through the magical forest night. Soon they were lost altogether, though Harry as he watched and waved them homeward, heard for some while a faint thread of song that trailed behind them like a ribbon.

He went yawning back to the house, pausing to shut the dogs in the stable. It might be one of those nights when he was too tired even to undress.

Sarah came down the stairs as Harry went indoors. Without pausing to think about it, he went and flopped against her and put his arms round her, knowing now that she was a good sister to have and never mind any bothers in the past.

"Hush," she said, though he had not spoken. "Listen, now. Grandda's not well. Maybe he's quite ill. I can't tell that too easy – he never will say how he feel."

"Tired. Just tired. That's all he is."

"We'll hope that, Harry." She gave him a gentle enough shove towards the stairs. "Get yourself to bed, do. You're near dropping."

"Aren't you, then?"

"Too much to think about," said Sarah. "Get on. We'll have to wait till morning. See how he go."

As he stumbled up the stairs, the best part of his pleasure in the evening drained right away. Harry remembered what he had been told of his own mother - how she might be there with them today if they had not lived so far from the town, if the doctor had only been able to get to them in time.

Chapter Eight

GRANDDA'

When Harry woke on Sunday morning, he woke late and with a jerk. He felt as if he had not been to sleep at all, for he had dreamed so much he was exhausted. He had had dreams of what was to happen to the old man, dreams of Mr Kingham, dreams of Sam and his boasts of living at Hoads while Harry was carted away and shut up in an orphanage. Half-awake, he thought he heard voices. He must have overslept really badly and Sarah was doing her best to wake him. Then he realised that Sarah was in his grandfather's room across the narrow landing. That meant, at least, that matters were no worse than they had been at midnight.

Because he was late and thought he could hear, now, the cows lowing as they waited for him, Harry was rather sorry that he had after all made the effort to get out of his clothes last night. But as he shook off the remains of his uncomfortable night, he realised that would have meant setting about the day's work in his one good shirt, so things were better as they were. As he pulled on his breeches and smock, Harry paused every now and again to listen. Grandda' and Sarah were arguing. Grandda' sounded a good deal stronger than he had done last night – a very good thing, too, except that he was using the improvement to be obstinate and Sarah was beginning to sound impatient.

"Leave me be and get about your business," Harry heard his grandfather say roughly. "You mind your manners, Sarah Hoad. I'll do what I want when I want. Give over fussing and whining."

Sarah might have snapped and grumbled in her time

but she had never whined. Harry expected her to reply sharply. But she contrived to answer calmly, saying only "There now" or "Let be" or some such soothy words. Then she left him and went downstairs, calling to Harry as she went.

"Get on your feet, do. You'm late. Come on down or get n'breakfast."

Harry gobbled his breakfast to get to the milking. On Sundays, for some reason, he always had a bite before starting work, though on any other old day he had to wait till the cows were back in the meadow. Why this should be, why they must wait uncomfortably on what was supposed to be the best day of the week, Harry had never properly discovered. Long ago he had asked Sarah why, and she had answered shortly, "Because it's Sunday, why else?"

"Ill," Sarah said, as she poured Harry's tea. "Grandda's ill. Not well at all. Keeps turning swimey. What's best I should do?"

"Be over it tomorrer."

"He's old. Old people stop being better. There's none lives for ever, you know that and so do I. We sh'd fetch a doctor."

"He'd go wild if you done that."

"I know it. Anyway – none'd come on a Sunday, I'd say. Doctors is respectable gentlemen. They'll all be in church."

Harry swallowed his tea too hot, burnt his tongue and burnt his throat. He wanted to get away, not only for the sake of the cows, but before Sarah said any more. He knew what she was talking about, warning him in that solemn way. She was trying to tell him that Grandda' might be going to die. It was a fine sunny morning. He did not want to think about such things, he did not want to think what happened next. If only he had Mrs Kingham to talk to – she would be sure, somehow, to make things seem easier. If Grandda' died, Sarah and Ben could be married; and that, Mrs Kingham would say, could only be a matter for rejoicing. But even Mrs Kingham would not be able to tell him what would happen next – what would happen next to Harry Hoad. And even Mrs Kingham, he had to admit, would not be able to banish the dread he was feeling now. For he was looking towards a time when there would no longer be a Farmer Hoad working among all the rest who took their living from the forest fringes, from the grazing and the ancient right that allowed them to cut wood and bracken. Harry had been told once how long there had been Hoads about the forest, but he had forgotten. His great-grandfather, his great-great-grandfather, perhaps even more greats . . . But he, Harry, would be the last Hoad in that place, for all the rest had chosen to go elsewhere. Only Luke, the best forest Hoad of them all, had not been given the choice.

"Hey up!" Harry called to his cows as he clattered the pails and shoved at the churns and behaved in every way as he felt a farmer should, slapping each milked cow lovingly on her great rump as she frisked past him towards the meadow.

It was indeed a most beautiful morning. The cows seemed to like it, too, racing over their pasture, flicking their tails and their ears, kicking up their heels. The air was very fine and there was that tilting of the season towards autumn that the harvest had signalled. At such a time the forest seemed poised on an invisible summit from which there could be only one descent, and that must be into winter. Winter, true winter, seemed far off to Harry as he stood almost until noon, watching his precious cows enjoying themselves, and trying not to listen to Sam Blagden's mocking voice echoing in his memory – "It's the orphanage for you, Harry Hoad!"

"Come to your dinner!" Sarah called, standing at the kitchen door. "What're you at? Come on and don't dally!"

Sarah's Sunday dinners were always her best. Nothing

was going right this Sunday, however. The harvest supper had used up even more than had been planned and they had to make do with what had been held back – a few slices of ham, some cake and a jelly that had not set properly and been considered unworthy of appearance at the supper. Somehow the way it sprawled on its dish was a measure of that day's despairs. Harry rose up from the table very nearly as hungry as when he sat down.

"What's for supper?" he asked, as the table was cleared.

That made Sarah laugh. "Crumbs and butter," she said.

Harry whistled up the two younger dogs and set out with them to the big pond where often there were swans settled for the summer. Usually there were two pairs of adult birds in any season and just now they would be caring still for their grey-feathered young. This was another place Harry had often visited with Luke, who had told him how swans mated for life so that a widowed bird might well stay solitary ever after. How much Luke had taught him and how much more he would know by now if only Luke had not been wrenched away! He crouched down at the water's edge, the dogs beside him, their ears hanging down as they looked into the water with him. There were minnows darting among the weed, almost a shoal of them – however many that might mean – it was the word Luke had always used. *Shoals o' trout, carp b'the shoal* . . . Luke had told Harry there had been great iron workings in this part of the forest and what they sometimes called a lake had been then a *hammer pond*. There had been a drop in level and a fiercely running tide that made power for the great hammer used to batter and shape the iron, smelted from the forest stone. This was one of the few stories Luke had told him that Harry had found hard to take in. Then one day in school, Mr Kingham told the same tale. It was too late by then to apologise to Luke for doubting him. And that brought Harry, crouching by the great pond on that wretched beautiful Sunday, back to his woes. Without either Luke or Mr Kingham he would surely be a dunce forever until he died.

When Harry got home, Sarah and Ben Rolfe were sitting together on the bench outside the kitchen door. The sun was warm on them. They were sitting hand in hand and Ben was leaning forward to look into Sarah's face as he talked. His manner was earnest and intent. What was he saying? Was it, *When shall we hope to marry?* or *How is the old man now?* or *What of young Harry? What of him for the future?*

Orphanage - orphanage - orphanage, rang in Harry's imagination as he went indoors. It might have been easier if he had been able to picture such a place. Where, for a start? In the town? Or in a country place where at least the wind might carry some smell of the forest? But since schools were in towns so, it seemed to him, must orphanages be. All the sounds would be different - boots on cobbles, wheels on cobbles, hooves on cobbles. Where would the cuckoo call? Would there be a window to lean through to hear in the dark the vixen crying and her mate replying? What birds sang in town gardens? There could be no deer, no badger, no squirrel or rabbit except in the great grounds of those richer near-town dwellers whose big family houses had each its own supplying farm - there at least familiar smells could be recognised . . .

Sarah came indoors suddenly and swiftly.

"Did Grandda' call? Did you hear'm, Harry?"

He had been too taken up with his own gloomy imaginings to hear anything. But as he shook his head, both heard the old man calling out from above stairs.

"I'll go," Harry said.

He bounded up the stairs, glad to know that Sarah had returned at once to Ben.

The old man was lying on the bed with his head flung back and a little sideways. He did not move immediately and for a second Harry thought that the call he and Sarah had heard must have been their grandfather's last. But then he moved, tossing himself on to one elbow and peering towards the door.

"Harry? That you, Harry?"

"Yes, Grandda'."

"Come here, boy. There's things got to be done."

Harry went to stand by the bed. He wondered if he should call Sarah. Better ask, he decided.

"Leave her be," his grandfather answered. "Ben Rolfe's come, en't he? Then let 'em be, let 'em be. Anyways – it's the cows need talking of."

Instantly, Harry was on his guard.

"What of'm?"

"Time they went."

Harry had been waiting for something of this sort, but he was still unprepared for it on this particular day.

"Why?"

"Still five, eh?"

"'Course there's five." If the old man could not remember that much he must be far gone. Whatever he might have decided could perhaps be ignored.

"Get on then, Harry," said Grandda' sharply, very much all there. "Tell me of 'm. How many in milk?"

Heather and Clover's just bin to Tomsetts. He'll have the calves, Mr Tomsett will – like you always said."

"Rightly so. What then?"

"Then there's Rosie and Dainty. Buttercup."

"Two o' them's the best part of four year old, as I recall it."

Harry nodded. Dainty, he meant, for one. She was a bit obstinate and he loved her perhaps less than the others.

"Time's come, then, boy. Sell'm. There'll be no Hoad in this place once I'm gone and Sarah's wed."

"Me," said Harry, hoping perhaps to raise at least a smile.

"You're only a boy – a boy. No good. Whyn't Luke here

still? Luke'd be a better farmer than any. None o' the rest was farmers – not proper. Only Luke and you, boy. You're years and years too young, you'll not be let stay. No sense in it, anyways."

"I'll get older – "

"Not in time, you wun't." Grandda' gave an un-expected chuckle. "I'd need to be a hundred and I never will be a hundred! Do's I say. Take the cows to market. What day's it? Anyways, next market's next week – always has bin. You see to it. Maybe you'm young but you'm sharp. Get 'em to market and bargain it out wi' the rest, eh? Get's much as you may. You c'n manage. Tell Sarah I say so. Get about it. No good dallying, Harry. Get it done. I must know it's bin done."

"Not Buttercup, eh, Grandda'? Need Buttercup for our own selves. Wun't we?"

"Take the lot and no grousing. It's change, that's what it is. Change." He moved angrily on the hard mattress and thumped at his pillow. "Do's I say and I'll die easy. Do's I say, like a good farmer's boy."

Chapter Nine

ST GILES'S MARKET

Harry stood among all the other farmers in the market place. He had stalled his cows as instructed by a fat red-faced fellow who would keep asking who Harry's master might be.

"I'm master today," said Harry. "These beasts is my beasts to sell as I choose."

"Watch out, then," said the man, grinning a bit. "A bargain's a bargain and there's many seeking one. See you don't get done." He turned away but then came back. "Better you save 'em till noon. What's not sold b'then goes to auction."

"Thanks very much," said Harry without a smile. "Maybe yes, maybe no."

At that the man shrugged, as if saying he had done his best to din sense into the silly young fool – the rest was up to him.

This was a special market, not just 'next week's' as the old man had told him. By chance it turned out to be that market, held yearly in this village, called St Giles's Market. It had been held here in this exact place for at least a hundred years, some said far longer. And so it might very well be, since it was named for a saint; saints, except for a few, had gone somewhat out of fashion. Giles was a good farmer's name, too, which surely meant that the saint had been a working man. The spot where the market – *fair* might be a better name – was always held, looked out over mile upon mile of meadowland, southward to the ever present downs, northward to the mysterious stretches of the weald, where the forest lay. There was therefore about the place a linking with times long past that gave it a flavour of its own. Numberless tales were told of happenings 'ten year ago (or twenty or seventy or three hundred) on St Giles's market day'.

It was customary to set up stalls on the market verges, and always there were gypsy vans alongside a small thicket, which was in fact named Romany Wood. Harry had only once before been to any market, let alone St Giles's, and now here he found himself, no mere strolling onlooker, but a stockman with beasts to sell. Looking around him he seemed to see nothing but guileful faces worn by men old enough to be his father. How would they treat him? Had he come here only to be cheated? Would they jeer at him, laugh and turn away from the idea of doing business with such a boy – or would their eyes light up greedily at the sight of one so young and therefore ignorant that he could surely be cheated with ease?

Harry had risen that morning even earlier than usual, got the milking over, and walked the distance in two hours with a bit over. It had rained the night before and the going, after a long dry spell, was thus made easier for man and beast. The rain had been steady and gentle, laying the dust, softening the surface without turning it to mud, which would have meant a good deal of hindering slippery stretches. The weather was still overcast at the start of the journey, though it was lifting at the edges as if the rain might well blow away. It was a good day for journeying, being neither too hot for the animals nor too cold for their drover. And it proved a good day for marketing as far as the general activities were concerned.

Because of the tradition of time and place there was an atmosphere of fellowship at St Giles's Market. Men shouted greetings to new arrivals, laughed at loud jokes and eyed the girls in a manner a long way from merely polite. There were more women present than there would have been at the ordinary weekly market. This was because of the many stalls selling such goods as spun wool, gingerbread, dolls and stuffed toys; rolls of woollen cloth for the making of jackets and breeches; cotton for petticoats and blouses or curtains and tablecloths. At weekly markets the wives and daughters were responsible for little more than eggs and butter and meat pies. Today they had come from far around and they were all making the most of the day out. There was a very good crowd there that day, and its shouting and general merriment was matched by the noise of the animals – cows, sheep, hens, geese all adding their cries to the hubbub. And in and out of the crowd the gypsy women weaved a way with their baskets of lavender bags and clothes pegs, and their soft persuasive voices offering to tell a fortune.

"Cross m'hand wi' silver, young sir. Tell if she love you true. Stay now, do. Where's that sixpence you promised . . . ?"

For Harry, just short of midday, it had been the loneliest morning of his life. Once or twice in the great crowd of strangers he caught sight of a forest face, but without being able to put a name to it. Once, far away on the fringes of activity, Harry thought he saw Mr Kingham. But Mr Kingham was no farmer and so could have little occasion to visit St Giles's Market. It was Harry's deep desire to speak with him, to learn what was happening to him and why he had left the school, that easily fitted his features on to some stranger.

Through all that long morning, no one spoke to Harry. No doubt they took him for a lad looking after his master's beasts and the master was nowhere to be seen. Now and again someone paused and inspected the cows and then passed on. Were they such poor things that they were not worth having? Harry would not leave his cows to go and discover how they compared with others. He was far too ignorant of how men behaved at cattle-markets to risk quitting his treasures for even a minute or two. He began to wonder what would happen next. Would he indeed have to put them to auction, letting them go to men he had never set eyes on, not knowing how they might be treated? He knew he would drive them the long way home rather than that. But what would his grandfather say to him then? What would Sarah say?

The auction had long started when a man came to Harry's pitch, paused a moment, then leant on the rail and considered the five cows in their stalls. It was not the first time Harry had noticed him and wondered if he would stop, but so far he had only paused briefly and then moved on. He was a youngish man, fair haired, with a good firm face, a steady eye and a strong mouth. He was dressed in a manner that suggested some upper farm servant - a steward, a bailiff or somesuch. As every decently dressed man with an air of authority was bound to remind Harry of Mr Kingham, this one was sure to do the same. If he was indeed interested in the cows, Harry trusted he might have the upright ways and honesty of the schoolmaster. He could not help feeling glad that here was no foresty man, for any forester was obliged to be wily, knowing very well what it was to be cheated and even better how to turn the tables.

"Tell me how they do," he said at last. "I see them well cared for. How do they repay that care? What's their yield? Do they calve easily? Can you point out their owner?"

"Me," said Harry.

The man smiled. "Yours, are they? You're a fairly young farmer, by the looks of you." He moved, then, among the cows, feeling their joints, inspecting their ears and eyes. "Well cared for indeed," he said. "And so you are their owner, you tell me."

"I cared for 'em since I were nine years old. My grandfather sent me wi' 'em. He'm old and sick and like to die. He tell me to sell 'em for my own."

"They do you credit - and I'd say you do your grandfather credit."

"Shall you take 'em, then, master?"

9. St Giles's Market

Over on the far side of the field there was much noise from the auction ring, where by now there was a good crowd looking on or bidding. The noise seemed to increase all the others, and the air was full of cries and talk and shouts, both men and women calling their wares, with dogs barking, cattle and sheep lowing or bleating, with goats, geese and hens coming in on a shriller note, and over all the auctioneer's gabbling chant and cries of "Done!" It seemed to Harry a savage noise, the noise of men fighting over bargains, and the bargains themselves, the animals, bellowing in fear as they were shoved and prodded and driven. It became clear to Harry then that he had better not sell his little herd, neither one nor all, if that was to be their treatment.

"Better after all I take 'em back home," he muttered.

"Don't be so hasty. What should your grandfather say to that? And you have not heard my answer. Will I take them, you ask me?"

At this precise moment Harry saw May running through the crowd towards him.

"Harry! Found you, then. You haven't sold 'em? Then Dad'll have them for sure. Soon's he heard, he would come here. Sarah never should've told how ill your Grandda's being."

"Why's he want 'em? He never kept cows afore."

"To go along with Hoads – what else? Soon's your poor old man dies, Hoads is firm promised to my father. It's true, Harry . . . But don't let him have 'em. He's a cruel man – and that I know well enough."

May had never said so much before. She could say no more for Ranger Blagden appeared through the crowd.

"There you are, Harry Hoad. And y'r cows along wi' you. Still for sale, I see. Good. Past her prime, every one but one. I'll gi' you forty-five pounds the five."

During all this, Harry's stranger had been standing in silence. Now he moved very slightly forward and put his hand on Harry's shoulder.

"Too late, I fear," he said. "These five cows, the property of John Hoad, have just now been sold to me."

Ranger Blagden gave his sneering laugh. "Then they'd best be *un*-sold, eh Harry? Speak up, now, and tell this fellow I'm an old friend. You know I'll not cheat you."

"Forty-five pounds proves otherwise," the first bidder said.

"Do it, indeed. I'm a cheat, then, am I? Look at they beasts, will you? One on'm looks twenty-year-old at the least."

"My offer, however, is seventy pounds, paid in cash here and now. Match that, if you care to."

"Match *seventy*? For that tired old lot?"

"Done, then!" cried the man; and he took Harry by the hand and shook it firmly.

Scarlet in the face, Ranger Blagden gobbled for words. May hung on to his arm and tried to soothe him – perhaps she feared he might knock his rival down and a terrible fight would follow, such things did happen on market days.

"My name is William Rainey," the stranger said to Harry. "Any day you need me, leave word at *The Forester's Arms*. Now – here's what I owe."

He pulled two small money bags from his deep jacket pocket, one full and the other empty. He transferred seventy gold sovereigns from the full to the empty, counting them out in tens. At the end of each ten he looked towards the Ranger with a lift of the eyebrow that seemed to say 'Contradict that, if you dare!' Then he wound its leather thong round the neck of the bag and tied it firmly. "Take that home to your grandfather," he said. "He will be pleased with you."

As Harry walked home, the gold coins were heavy round his neck – May had found a piece of string to hang the little bag on and as he walked it banged against his chest.

"The poor old man," May said. "He'll be so glad you

done well."

Harry did smile slightly, but it was a poor effort. All he could think of was those five cows being driven away by William Rainey and a lad who had appeared from nowhere to give him a hand. Never again the sight of them in the meadow, the smell of them in the byre, the warmth of them as he settled with stool and pail in the dusky light of the milking shed. Harry had been a farmer's boy for most of his life but though there had to be changes in that time among the cattle, a newcomer would take an old name – and so there had always been a Buttercup, always Rosie and the rest. Now those names were taken from him, it was almost as if he had lost his own name, too.

May had left her father to drive the trap home on his own. She walked silently beside Harry all the long way from St Giles's Market to Hoads Farm. There seemed nothing more that either of them need say.

Only as the farm came into view did Harry realise what other changes must result from what was soon to come. Because he had lost his five treasures, he must soon lose more. He understood at last, to the full, what Sarah and May had often tried to make clear to him – that Hoads were only tenants of the Lord of the Manor and as such had no rights to the property once the chief tenant was gone. Even if Luke had still been with them, an obvious heir, it would have depended on the Lord whether he would be allowed to succeed his grandfather. Even if Luke had still been with them – Ranger Blagden could have been handed the farm.

A terrible urgency took Harry. Without even a word of thanks or farewell to May, he rushed down the track and pelted across the yard to the house, shouting for Sarah.

"Awake is he? I sold 'em! He'll be that glad I sold 'em well. Best tell him quick!"

Sarah seemed likely to check him, but changed her mind and let him go. He dashed into his grandfather's room and across to the bed.

"Grandda'! Look! Look what I got! Look what I brought you home 'stead of cows!"

He pulled out the fat purse and untied it and slid a little cascade of gold into his palm, so that the coins sang together.

The old man was lying on his back, very still, but with a look of such delighted cunning on his shrivelled old face that Harry laughed out loud.

"How much? How much 'e pay?"

"Seventy pound, Grandda'!"

"Seventy? *Seventy*? Then you kep' 'em from Blagden – he'd never pay seventy."

"Mr William Rainey, it were – that's who give me seventy."

For a second or two his grandfather said nothing. Then he began to chuckle.

"You done well, young Harry. Knew you would. True forest farmer, Harry Hoad – true farmer, eh? That Blagden'll be sore as nettle stings! He'll be raging and howling. Good, I say. Good."

And rather slowly but very firmly, he gave Harry a delighted wink.

Chapter Ten

FARMER'S BOY

Harry came back up the cellar steps carrying more cider, as Sarah had told him to. Above him he heard the great chatter and argument of thirty or so people gathered in the parlour, spilling into the kitchen and passageway. Beyond the windows the rain poured down. Not much more than two hours ago they had all stood round Grandda's grave listening to the parson - Mr Goodhew, unfortunately - praying in a sing-song voice so unlike any real person that Harry would have been glad to push him into the grave along with the coffin. It was only when they got to the farm and settled down together that Grandda' was spoken of as he had truly been - a quick-tempered, sturdy forest man whose troubles had been many but had never dimmed his spirit, whose courage had not been broken, whose affections had been few but deeply centred - his wife, his son, his grandsons, Luke and Harry, his granddaughter, Sarah; the last a little grudging.

"He never did reckon much of the rest of us," one of today's visitors had told Harry.

And yet how many had come to see him on his way from life. How had the news got round? Ben Rolfe had carried it to the Manor, of course, so Aaron and Martha had been given leave for that whole day. But no one had discovered how Mark and Rebecca had learnt of it - Mark away on the coast at his fishing, Rebecca by now somewhere on the borders of Kent. Mark and his wife, Alice, came with two children; Rebecca and her husband, Bert, had brought their twin sons, Freddy and Martin, and Rebecca had another baby on the way. Of those near

enough to come once more into their old home, only one
sister, Mary, was missing – and since the last that had
been heard of her was that she had been taken ill, no one
spoke of her very much. Besides the family, there were
friends and neighbours, not to mention Alice's parents
and Bert's brothers and sister with their wives and husband. By now they all knew that Ranger Blagden had
been granted the tenancy of Hoads Farm. Wisely, he had
not attended the funeral, but May had come, as always to
be helpful to Sarah. Sam was there, too, which Harry
could have done without, for he kept staring at Harry, for
once without a word, not even *orphanage*. And where
Harry was to start thinking of what was to happen next
he could not imagine, for all was at sixes and sevens.
Though he had known Grandda' must die soon and that
then the whole of life would change, the change seemed
now too great to contemplate. For over all was the fact
that no one, so far, had spoken of what was to happen
next to him.

As Harry carried the cider into the parlour, the talk
that had been so loud and busy suddenly wavered, hesitated, then died altogether. He found himself on the
threshold with all those pairs of eyes turned towards
him. He knew at once without the least possible doubt
that they had been discussing him while he was out of
the way. They had been wondering what was to become
of him, where he should go, how he should live now that
he would have no home save what any one of them could
offer him. He knew enough about making a living to
know also that in the households of fishermen and forest-
ers even one extra mouth could be an impossible burden.
Sarah would not desert him but she would marry Ben
now that her own home would no longer be hers. Would
His Lordship allow his coachman to take his young
brother-in-law to live with him? No one had offered any
opinion in Harry's hearing, but no doubt that was one
side of the business they had been talking about while he

was fetching the cider.

He lugged the heavy jars forward into the parlour.

"I thought best get up two," he said to Sarah.

They must all have been glad that the silence and staring was broken, for a considerable chatter broke out instantly.

"Two's needed, all right," cried Sarah. "Give's a hand, do, Ben. Every glass I see need filling."

That set the conversation going even faster and louder and Harry found himself the centre of all their concern.

"Here, then, Harry - where've you left your glass?"

"Drink up and cheer up, Harry boy."

"Here's my own Harry - named'm for you," cried his brother Mark. "How's that, then? Here now, young Harry, here's Uncle Harry to talk t'you."

The child was pushed forward. He and Harry stared at one another and looked foolish - for Uncle Harry did not know what one said to a nephew, while little Harry hardly knew yet how to say anything. And all the time, the silly encounter was made to last by grown-ups glad of a diversion, who laughed and made stupid remarks about likenesses, and anyone'd know they were related; and so on. There was Sam at the far end of the room gobbling all he could get hold of but never taking his eyes off Harry. As Harry saw it, there was one word written all over his stupid face - of course it was the word *orphanage*.

Like many another funeral, where grief and sadness are at first settled over all faces and eyes are downcast, the gathering had turned into a cheerful reunion party. When Mark and Rebecca were young they had of course had friends - and here were some of them who had not been encountered for many years. How strange to see childhood companions grown to wives and husbands with sons and daughters, and to talk at length of others who were not there but were not forgotten . . .

That moment of awkwardness was now past and Harry found himself moved from one to another of the guests, as though indeed he was an object of concern and even distress to them – none there but would be willing to do the very best for him – if they were able. But not one spoke of what was about to happen – the actual handing over of the farm, which could not in reason be more than a few weeks away, and what might follow then.

Gradually the afternoon passed. The guests began to rise and say their farewells to Sarah and to one another. Then there were wishes for everyone's good fortune, hopes that there might be meetings between one and another in the future – no doubt they were thinking that Sarah's wedding could not be far ahead. It was very unlikely that anything less than a wedding or a funeral could gather so many of them together after long parting. That Grandda' was gone and life could never be the same for at least two of their number seemed, by the time of farewells, to be calmly accepted. More important to them just then was the fact that his death had brought about a day of reunions that would long be remembered.

Sarah stood by the door to wave away the guests. Harry stood by her and she had her arm across his shoulders as if to comfort and reassure him. When the last guest had gone, then surely they must face the future, whatever it might be. As they all moved away now from the house, they were still talking and laughing, and when they reached the gate they stood about, unable to say a final goodbye. Mark had brought his family in a borrowed trap. The nearest neighbours said Rebecca should come to them, and in the morning they would get out the farm cart and take her and her family home to Kent.

"Where's May?" Harry asked Sarah.

"She went to say goodbye . . . Here she come now." Sarah's voice rose. "She's in some state, Harry!"

May ran towards them, calling their names. She looked quite wild, her face white, her eyes staring. Sarah ran towards her and caught her close.

"There – there, my dawlin. Whatever happen?"

"Sarah – oh Sarah . . . Harry, listen do! Mr Kingham – Mr Kingham come here!"

"Where? Where is'n?" Harry turned to run in search of him, but May caught his arm.

"Wait! I'll tell you. I'll tell you . . ."

By that time she was crying half hysterically, so that Sarah tried hard to calm her. But May's tale had to be told, however it might hinder Harry. Mr Kingham had come with news of Luke. Those friends and fellow workers in the cause of prisoners were home in England on a visit.

"They'll be here till autumn," May said. "Sarah! Luke's been sent to work for 'em on their farm. No, no – he'll never come home – but they'll take me with 'em when they go. We'll be married after all! Luke and me'll be man and wife after all!"

As the news got home to Harry, he saw that some of the guests, too, had realised something was happening. Some turned back and gathered round May and Sarah, and the tale was told all over again to cries of sympathy and amazement. Once more Harry was forgotten, and he began to shove his way out of the crowd that hemmed him in. May had spoken to Mr Kingham – but where? Had he been here in person as she said? And if so, where was he now? Harry could only think that he had come and gone and he was filled with the despair of any grown man. Indeed he put his hands over his face and stood a second almost shaking with disappointment.

Then he heard Mr Kingham's voice.

"There you are, Harry. Here I am, you see, as promised. Though I fear we have come on a day of sadness for you all."

Mrs Kingham was at her husband's side. "He was a good old man," she said. "He had much to bear."

Just for a second Harry did not answer, for he was remembering that wicked wink Grandda' had given him

– then closed his eyes for good. But there were more immediate things to think about. What had Mr Kingham meant by 'as promised'?

At this moment Sarah realised who had arrived and came to greet them. She was looking by this time rather pale and tired, and she was fussed at their arrival in the midst of such confusion.

"May told us," she said.

They had not realised about the funeral party, Mr Kingham said, or they would have waited until the next day.

"But good news is best told at once, I think you will agree. May we come in? There are other matters to speak of."

This sounded mysterious enough, but by now Harry had seen the trap standing in the yard. It was a light and rather smart affair and would have needed a skilful driver to bring it over the forest track that was full of ruts and bumps. That driver was in fact standing by the horse's head, inspecting its mouth as though he feared he might have been over firm and the bit could have caused some damage. The man who stood there, absorbed in what he was doing, Harry had seen last at St Giles's Market – William Rainey, who had bought five cows from Harry and paid seventy gold sovereigns for them . . .

The arrival of Mr and Mrs Kingham sped the last guests on their way. It was hardly to be expected that gentry folk would come to take part in a gathering of farming folk, therefore they must have come for some special purpose. In ones and twos they said their farewells, the women bobbed, the men touched their foreheads, the children looked bemused. It was May, now flushed and tear-stained, who saw them all on their way. Because of the newcomers, a boisterous departure became a very quiet and mannerly one.

"We shall not keep you long, I think," Mr Kingham said.

"But these other matters must be related."

Sarah had ushered them into the parlour. The room was in a pretty fair muddle, plates and glasses and mugs on every surface, crumbs on the floor, chairs all over the place.

"Clear up a bit, Harry," Sarah said, almost blushing that the Kinghams should see such chaos. "Then go and help May in the kitchen."

"No, no," Mr Kingham said. "Harry must be present while we talk. Pray leave the clearing – it is of no importance. Let us sit down quietly."

Sarah waited until the Kinghams were seated, then perched on the very edge of a kitchen chair and waited. She looked puzzled, even worried, anxious. Because she was nervous she spoke first, which ordinarily she would not have done in this situation.

"May tell us a wonderful tale, sir. Shall your friends truly do this for her?"

"There need be no difficulty. Only her father may object. But we shall talk him round – shall we not, my dear?" he said to his wife, smiling.

"Oh indeed, yes. It is never impossible to talk such a person into agreement." And she smiled in her turn and nodded to Sarah. "But now let us speak of Harry."

"Of course," Sarah said. "Harry." She glanced up at him as he stood stiffly beside her chair. Each was as puzzled as the other.

Mr Kingham frowned very slightly.

"Did you get no message of mine from young Sam Blagden, Harry? That in due course I would be coming to see you?"

"He never say so, sir. Only said there'd be n'more school."

"Not there," Mr Kingham said. "Not that school. I am to have my own school. I have a house left by my father. It is to be there. He said nothing of that?"

"Oh no!" Sarah cried. "Harry'd have told me. He

thought you'd gone away. Didn' you, Harry?"

Harry nodded. He did not speak for fear of saying the wrong thing. Did Mr Kingham mean that he, Harry Hoad, would be allowed to go to this new school? Where was it? Perhaps too far away? In any case, they never would let him out from that orphanage to go to a different school.

Mr Kingham was saying to Sarah that with the house there went a very pleasant small estate.

"Some three hundred acres. Very well situated. The house of suitable size." He glanced at his wife and smiled. "And then there is the home farm."

"We need help there," put in Mrs Kingham, nodding.

"Yes, indeed, my dear. We shall take a few lads to learn farming as well reading and writing. There will be quarters for them. They will in fact earn their keep by caring for various farm affairs."

"Such as milking," said Mrs Kingham.

"Such as milking," Mr Kingham agreed. "So - what do you think, Harry? I hope you will agree to be our first pupil - for there are the cows, you see - the five cows that have been so long in your care - that my farm manager, William Rainey, so cleverly found waiting for him at St Giles's Market."

"Buttercup . . ." muttered Harry.

"How are the rest called?"

"Rosie, Dainty, Heather, Clover . . ." He saw them as he named them. He began to smile.

"Well, well - we must learn to know which is which. So shall you like to come and care for them?"

Harry gazed at Mr Kingham. He was not quite sure what was being said, so extraordinary it seemed after all his worrying. He glanced at Mrs Kingham, and she nodded and smiled.

"I know he will come," she said. "I trust him to come. Like the cows, Harry, we need you!"

Now Harry looked at Sarah. She was smiling as he had

hardly ever seen her smile. Her life, too, was straighten-
ing itself as they talked. But she did not press or badger
him. Perhaps she was recalling the many, many times,
before Ben Rolfe came into her life, that she had snapped
and nagged. But as Harry himself seemed struck dumb,
she said at last,

"That seem good to you, then, Harry?"

He nodded. He moved to her and put his arms round
her, as neither of them would ever have expected him to
do, least of all with visitors present. Then he moved away
and went towards Mrs Kingham, but did not know what
to say. Too much was changing, too much to be taken in,
let alone properly understood. He felt shy and stupid,
and wished he had not put his arms round Sarah, as if he
were a child not a farmer's boy.

"There now," said Mrs Kingham. "I knew we had the
right answer. We'll expect you tomorrow."

So then Harry went to Mr Kingham, who stood up and
faced him. Very solemnly and firmly, they shook hands.

Now the trap was turning away from Hoads Farm that
soon would carry a different name, while Sarah and
Harry waved and William Rainey flicked his whip in
farewell as they drove off.

Sarah peered into Harry's face, that was still solemn
with amazement.

"That as you like it, Harry?"

He nodded. Perhaps from wherever the new place lay
there would be some view of the forest that had been
home.

"I'll still be a farmer's boy," he said.

"That's good, en't it?"

He nodded, smiling at last. "That's good," he said.
"Grandda'd say so."